One Lucky Girl

One Lucky Girl

SANTINA S. PROCTOR

"Find someone who knows how *lucky* they are to have you."

Contents

I dedicate this book to my journey: to the girl I once was, the woman I am now, and the woman I continue to grow into, recognizing that God's plans always surpass my own.
-Santina S. Proctor

High School Sweethearts

1

"No, no, no. Mimi, please tell me there aren't two lines!"

"I wish I could, girl, but it's two lines, and the lines are dark as hell!"

"This can't be life! I am not ready to be a mom, and Brenton is not ready. He has scholarship offers, and I have plans. Big plans!"

"Sharae, you are tripping. No one is expecting you to have a baby at 17. I'll give you the number of the clinic I went to last year. All you need is about $500 and someone to drive you."

Mimi was talking, but my mind was in a trance. I can't believe a baby is growing inside of me. I want to be a mom, but not right now. I'm too young, and my dad will kill me.

How is it going to look with him laying hands on everybody and his baby girl can't keep her legs closed? It's not like I'm a hoe. Brenton is the only boy I've been with, but that doesn't matter. All everyone will see is another teen mom. Then how am I going to go to college with a kid? FUCK! Why didn't I make Brenton wear a condom? I tried to talk to my dad about birth control, but he said, "You don't need birth control when you're celibate." I didn't dare tell my dad I hadn't been celibate since my 16th birthday.

Mimi convinced me that I should lose my virginity on my 16th birthday to show a sign of becoming a woman. Mimi has been my best friend since the 4th grade. I remember Mimi walking into Mrs. Dodd's class wearing a Punky Brewster shirt, colorful leggings, and Timberland boots. Mrs. Dodd introduced her to the class and informed us that Mimi was from Brooklyn, New York. Some of the kids began to snicker and make remarks about her boots. I thought Mimi looked like a "Fly Girl" dancer on the TV show *In Living Color*. Her long hair was pulled up into a ponytail by red, purple, and green scrunchies.

I raised my hand and asked Mrs. Dodd if Mimi could sit next to me. Ever since that spring day at Westside Elementary, Mimi and I have been clique-tight. We've never even argued. My house was a safe place for Mimi. Her mom's boyfriend was a drunk who chose to beat on her mother whenever he felt like it, and her stepbrother would always accidentally come into the bathroom while Mimi was getting out of the shower.

I lived through Mimi's stories of Bodegas and riding the city bus as a kid in a big city. She always told me that we would visit Brooklyn together and that I could meet her real dad. She said he was a big drug dealer, and she had to move from New York because there were threats to her family's life. Mimi's dad sent her and her mom to Florida and told Mimi that no one was going to run him out of his city. I imagined Mimi's dad to be like Nino Brown from the movie New Jack City.

Sadly, the summer we were entering middle school, Mimi's dad was arrested, and on his way to the precinct, he was murdered. Mimi told me some crazy stories about how the police set her dad up to be murdered. I still wanted to visit New York.

"Sharae, *hello*, earth to Sharae!"

Mimi snapped her fingers as she tried to get my attention.

"Give me the number, Mimi, and I'ma need a ride."

The next two weeks seemed like two months. As soon as I found out I was pregnant, the morning sickness started. The first morning of throwing up, I was able to make my dad believe that I had food poisoning. The night before he insisted that I accept his girlfriend's offer to cook us dinner.

It had been my dad and I forever, and I was not interested in having any woman pretend to be my mom. I only wanted to give Caprice a chance because I was leaving for college in a few months, and I didn't want my dad to be lonely. Luckily, her food was horrible, so food poisoning was not too far-fetched. The other days, I took nausea pills. I wasn't keeping the baby, so there was no need for me to be careful about what I ingested.

"Sharae Smith."

I stood up, and Mimi gave me a half-smile. I don't remember much about my procedure. I just remember the room being really cold, the doctor telling me to relax my legs, and a loud suctioning sound. The nurse held my hand and wiped the tears from my eyes. I didn't say a word. I lay on the table with my eyes open, staring at the ceiling. Strangely, there were pictures of Disney princesses painted on the ceiling. Mimi was waiting for me in the lobby.

As soon as we got in the car, Mimi blasted the radio and started to rap along with the baddest female rapper in the game, Trina. I laid the seat of her Honda Civic back and held my stomach. I didn't want to have a baby, but I didn't want to be a murderer either. I should've told Brenton. Maybe he would've had a plan. Maybe his parents would've taken me in.

As we turned off Jimmy Ann Drive, I could see my dad in our front yard. His bald head was shining from a mile away. My dad was often mistaken for Emmitt Smith. With his bald head, chocolate skin, and short stature, I could see how people made the comparison. He was no athlete, though, but he was a faithful member of the YMCA and could outrun someone half his age. My dad enjoyed watching all sports, but outside of bowling, he had no other interest in participating.

"Hi, Mr. Andre," Mimi said in her high-pitched voice.

My dad was watering our grass.

"Hey girls, where are y'all coming from?" he asked.

"Oh, we went to the gym to get in some extra conditioning before the track meet on Saturday."

My dad was all about hard work, so I knew that was an excuse he would love to hear.

"That's the right mindset, Sharae. You can't be in first place and not give first place effort."

I gave her two thumbs up and told Mimi I would catch up with her later.

"Dad, I am exhausted. After I shower, I'll be napping."

I thought I was going to be able to nap, but all I could do was cry. I cried because I felt alone. I cried because I wished I had a mom to talk with about this. I cried because I knew that God knew what I did. Brenton didn't know, and my dad didn't know, but God did.

I grabbed the Bible my mother gave me out of my nightstand and turned to Romans 3:23, "*For all have sinned and fall short of the glory of God.*" Christians are always trying to find a way to justify their sins, and I am no different.

I finally drifted off and dreamed of my unborn child. It was a girl. Brenton was so happy, and our parents weren't ashamed. I looked into my baby's bassinet, and she was beautiful. She reminded me of Princess Jasmine from the movie Aladdin.

Three Months Later

2

The moment has finally come. Everyone filled the Daytona Beach Ocean Center. I had a major plan that seemed to be foolproof, and so did Brenton. We both had full-ride scholarships to Norfolk State University in Virginia. We both dominated in track and excelled academically.

"Put your hands together as we welcome the class of 2001 Valedictorian, Sharae Smith!"

Everyone clapped. The lights were so bright that I could barely see any faces in the audience, but I could hear my dad blowing his bullhorn. The same one he used at every track meet, every debate, or any other activity I participated in. My dad always showed up. I know it wasn't easy for him to be a single parent, but he never complained. I heard him pray many nights that God would guide him so that he could guide me.

"Good evening, class of 2001!" I spoke into the mic clearly and concisely.

I reminisced on the times we shared over the past four years and gave a few hints of how Senior

Skip Day was one to remember.

"And as I close, I want each of you to know that we made it. We defeated the odds, and whatever we choose after this, it's up to us. On three, *Buc Pride Never Dies*. One, two, three...!"

The crowd erupted in an uproar as I walked back to my seat. I scanned the room, and I made eye contact with my dad. He clapped once and pointed to the sky. He started making that gesture soon after my mother died. He always reassured me that we weren't alone and that she was watching us.

Graduation night was a blast. Brenton and I had a joint cookout at my house, which of course brought the whole class of 2001 out and some underclassmen. The smell of BBQ filled the air, and music flooded the streets. Everyone loved my dad, so the neighbors allowed us to block off the entire street. Brenton and I had our very own block party.

I saw my dad, and Mr. Brothers, Brenton's dad talking casually. They grew up together and were best friends. I remember when my mother was dying when I was only seven years old. Mr. Brothers was at our house seemingly every day with Brenton and his mom, Mrs. Kim. The day my mother took her last breath, I sat beside her hospital bed with my dad and the Brothers' family, including Brenton. The sun shone brightly that day off of my mother's light brown skin. She was at peace.

Brenton and I had no choice but to become friends. We started by doing our homework together, and then it turned into us playing hide and seek. Before you knew it, we were two 10-year-olds secretly kissing and hunching on one another. Our parents knew that we wanted to be more than friends, so when we turned 14 years old, one month apart, they agreed to allow us to "date."

There wasn't much to our dating, just being able to spend time at one another's house while an adult was home or being dropped off at the movies or skating rink together. Finally, on my 16th birthday, our parents trusted us enough to date in private and chauffeur ourselves around.

"Are you sure about this?" Brenton spoke softly as he looked me in the eyes and unlatched my bra strap.

"I've never been so sure about something in all of my life."

I was lying to Brenton. I was terrified and unsure. I loved him, and we had been together for the past two years, but I promised my dad and God that I would wait until marriage before giving away my virginity.

I closed my eyes as I sang along to Aaliyah's lyrics playing in the background. Brenton was gentle. I almost couldn't believe that I was also his first.

He slowly spread my legs apart with his leg as he positioned himself on top of me. I could feel his warm lips on the nape of my neck. His breathing was deep but slow. I felt pressure and a moment of discomfort, but that soon turned into pleasure. Brenton's heart began to beat faster, and he quietly moaned. He whispered that he loved me and collapsed on top of me. I looked at the clock that sat on my bedroom nightstand, and what seemed like hours and hours was only twenty minutes.

"You're supposed to climax also."

"How am I supposed to do that?"

I had no idea what sex was supposed to be like, and I was supposed to feel something beyond the connection I already felt. I wasn't curious in that area of my life, and not having a mom, there were no sex talks. My dad barely knew what to tell me once I started my menstrual cycle. My 7th-grade guidance counselor is who I confided in after going to the bathroom and noticing brown gunk in my panties. She reassured me that I didn't poop myself and called my dad. The wall of menstrual pads looked like the walls in Jericho as my dad and I stood in silence, trying to decide which product was best for me. Thankfully, a random lady in Kmart helped, and every month my dad would place a bag of pads outside of my bedroom door.

"Get on top of me."

I got on top of Brenton and pretended that I was winding to a reggae beat. I started to feel something that I had never felt and before I knew it, I had no control. My back was arched, and I was screaming Brenton's name. He held onto my waist so that I couldn't raise my hips. And that is when I became an addict.

***

"Hey, boo, help me get some more sodas out of the house."

As soon as Brenton got into the house, I pushed him into our guest bathroom. I pulled up my short skirt, and he didn't hesitate to pull my panties to the side. Brenton entered me quickly, and within three minutes, we were both satisfied. I pulled down my skirt while Brenton pulled up his pants. We were back at our graduation party before anyone could miss us. It was common that Brenton and I would sneak away and have quick moments of pleasure. We were addicted to each other. We still didn't use condoms, but I was able to convince Brenton that the pull-out method was okay, and I learned how to track my ovulation, so no more scares for us.

"Sharae, come here, baby girl."

My dad reached out his arm. I ran up to him and placed his arm around my shoulder. My dad began to tell me how proud of me he was, how I helped him as much as he helped me, and that he would miss me. Tears began to well up in his eyes, and his voice got shaky.

"Dad, I love you forever, and this is only the beginning of our lifetime journey."

We hugged tightly and cried in one another's arms. This embrace seemed longer than others, and for some reason, I knew that things were officially different between my dad and me. As we let go of one another, Caprice began to rub my father's back.

Caprice was a good woman, and she genuinely loved my dad. She wasn't one of the women flaunting around when my mother first passed, pretending that they were so in love with God and just wanted the best for my dad. She wasn't a member of our church at all. Caprice is a hairstylist that my father found at the barbershop where he gets his haircut. He says Caprice overheard him talking about how he was having a hard time maintaining my hair, and she offered to do my first style for free. Caprice has been styling my hair for the last 10 years. She has magic hands. She doesn't just specialize in one type of hair. She can do everything.

After eight years of being my hairstylist, my dad finally realized that Caprice was really fine, like Vanessa Williams, and that she loved him. So, for the past two years when you saw Andre, you saw Caprice. She even became a member of our church. I don't know if my dad and Caprice have had sex because she has never spent the night at our home. I thought that was weird, but my dad said he didn't want to give me a bad example. I wouldn't have judged my dad, especially since I was bending over and lifting my skirt every chance that I got. I was hoping that my dad would propose to Caprice by now. He is going to need a woman in the home after I am gone.

Summer has come and gone. My dad, Caprice, and I went to the Dominican Republic for seven days, and that's when the magic happened. My dad proposed to Caprice on the beach and had secretly flown in her mother, father, her best friend Lisa, and her husband. It was so special. Caprice, of course, said yes.

I love Caprice. She didn't want a big, glamorous wedding and refused to let the church treat her like a spectacle. My dad had a simple ceremony that the entire congregation attended, but the wedding party was small. It included me, Lisa, and Mr. Brothers. The junior pastor married my dad, and the food was catered by my mother's best friend, Angel. Angel is my godmother, and it helped me a lot mentally that she was okay with Caprice. Life was working out great despite me not having my mother.

College Life

3

Virginia was definitely not Florida. I still wasn't too far away from the beach, but Virginia Beach was nothing like Daytona Beach. There was no Black College Reunion or Spring Bling. There was a college week, but the police were so heavy and racist that it wasn't as much fun.

The HBCU experience was good for me. *Behold, the Green and Gold*! Norfolk State Spartans were everything I needed as a college student.

Brenton and I stayed on campus until our senior year, and then we got an apartment together. Neither one of us decided to pledge to a sorority or fraternity. Not that we thought anything against it, but we were student-athletes, and both had gotten part-time jobs. I worked part-time for a real estate firm as an assistant, and Brenton worked at the YMCA as a personal trainer. Our sexual addiction to one another only increased once we moved in together.

We found a cute, little, one-bedroom apartment in downtown Norfolk off of Granby

Street, not too far from the university. It was above a restaurant that served the best pasta and played jazz music. I grew to love Ella Fitzgerald, Duke Ellington, and the other jazz greats.

I wish the pounds I had put on came from the pasta, but nope, I was pregnant, again. I refused to ever have another abortion. I still had nightmares of the first one, and every suctioning sound made me think of the baby that I murdered.

Brenton and I were one semester from graduation, and a baby was not going to stop our plans. Although I was going to graduate with a degree in nursing, I was planning to become a real estate agent. I hadn't told my dad my bright idea, but the true wealth I desired was going to come from real estate. I had already passed the real estate exam and was learning all I could as I worked as an assistant. Brenton wanted to become a full-time personal trainer, but he was too afraid to let his parents down, so he accepted an offer as a physical therapist at a local nursing home.

This time, I didn't have to tell Brenton that I was pregnant. He was so in tune with my cycle that he said something after two months that we had sex every day.

"Sharae, when were you going to tell me?"

"Tell you what?"

I pretended to act as if I didn't know what Brenton was asking about.

"About the baby. My baby."

"I didn't know how, and I'm not sure I want to keep it."

"What do you mean? We aren't getting rid of our baby."

"I won't have another abortion, but adoption is a possibility."

I hadn't considered adoption, but things were rolling off my tongue with ease.

"Another? When did you have an abortion? Why did you kill my baby?"

Anger rose in Brenton. I had never seen him upset or angry.

"I'm sorry."

Tears began to fall as I spoke to Brenton.

"You're sorry? Yeah, you are sorry. You're sorry, and you're selfish!"

Brenton yelled at me as he laced up his running shoes. Before I could respond, he was out the door.

I decided not to chase Brenton. I knew he needed time to not only digest that he lost a baby but that I was pregnant again. I stood naked in our bathroom, gazing at my reflection in the mirror. There was a natural glow to my skin. My short, natural hair was twisted into two strands, and the auburn color was beginning to fade. I caressed my boobs and slowly moved down to my stomach. I turned sideways and poked my stomach out a little to see how I would look with a baby bump. I imagined my small 5'3" frame wobbling as I carried life inside of me.

I must have fallen asleep because I woke up to Brenton turning me onto my stomach, spitting on my ass crack, and ramming his penis inside. I wanted to scream, but I couldn't. The initial pain turned into a sickening pleasure.

Brenton was slurring his words, and mixed with tears were a few *'selfish bitches'* and *'whys.'* After about ten minutes, Brenton collapsed on top of me. I slid from under him, and he began snoring softly. I ran some bath water, and the water stung my butthole. I relaxed my back against the bathtub and closed my eyes. Brenton came in shortly after.

"Sharae, I'm sorry. I shouldn't have treated you that way. I am just confused and afraid," Brenton said with sincerity in his voice.

I grabbed his hand and placed it on my stomach.

"What do you want to do?" I asked.

"I'm not ready. We're not ready. Adoption or abortion?" Brenton asked.

"I don't want a child in this world looking like us, and we aren't taking care of it."

Brenton responded softly, "Abortion it is."

I made an appointment the next day for the abortion, but this time I chose to use the pill method. There was no way I could endure the suctioning sound again.

The morning of my appointment, I sat on the bed and watched Brenton get dressed. I admired his physique. He was 6'1" with caramel brown skin. His eyes always seemed to pierce my soul. He had the sexiest legs, and his back had just the right amount of definition. Brenton kept his hair in a low fade with a taper. I knew once we decided to have kids that they would be beautiful, just like Princess Jasmine.

"Sharae Smith!?"

I stood up and followed the nurse. This time, I was given two pills. I was instructed to take the first pill now and to take the second pill in 24 hours. The nurse explained that I would feel cramping and that the tissue would pass.

Brenton was waiting for me. This time, no music was playing. Only silence. I could see a tear escape Brenton's face as he tried hard not to blink. I didn't cry this time. I was angry.

Both Brenton's parents and mine came for graduation. It was such a great time. I couldn't believe that our graduation day had finally come. Life was happening so fast - too fast. There was no big graduation party this time, only our family and us eating at Aberdeen Barn off of Northampton Blvd.

"So, Sharae, when do you sit for your NCLEX?" My dad asked energetically.

I didn't want to tell my dad that I wasn't planning on taking the nursing exam, but I had no choice.

"Dad, I've decided on a new career path."

The table talk fell quiet.

Caprice shifted in her seat and began to rub my dad's back. I was glad that she was there.

"I am waiting for your bright idea, Sharae."

"Well, Dad I've gotten my real estate license, and I am planning on becoming the number one selling agent. I have dreams of selling luxury homes."

I swallowed hard and waited for my dad to respond.

"I trust you, Sharae, but I still want you to take the NCLEX. Schedule the test, and I'll pay for it. There is no need to have a degree if you don't follow through."

"Thanks for understanding, Dad, and I'll schedule the test on Monday."

Brenton squeezed my hand and smiled. We had discussed how I would tell my dad my plans, and he knew that I was nervous about it. Thankfully, my dad was an easygoing guy and accepted my decision. I didn't want to disappoint my dad, so I was more than willing to take the nursing exam.

Brenton and I both decided to wait until June to go full force into adulthood as workers. I studied for the NCLEX endlessly, and Brenton went home to Florida to spend some time with his parents. At the end of May, I passed the exam without fault, and Brenton returned home to our home.

Adulting

4

I couldn't sleep. I was so excited to finally work full-time as a real estate agent. I woke up early Monday morning and fixed coffee. I wasn't a coffee drinker, but my mentor Renee always had a cup of coffee in her hand, and she closed deals, so I thought it might help.

"Ugh, Sharae, what kind of coffee is this?" Brenton said as he spit coffee from his mouth into the kitchen sink.

I laughed because I had no idea how to make coffee.

"Um, baby, I don't know. Are there certain types of coffee?"

Brenton scooped me up and sat me on a small space on our kitchen counter. He snuggled his nose into my neck, which made me feel giddy.

"I'm proud of you, Sharae. For real, girl, you're doing what you want to do."

"Thanks, babe, but you know you can too. We're young with no kids. This is the time to live our dreams without worry."

"No kids, damn Sharae, we were supposed to have two kids by now."

Brenton's voice began to fade, and I knew that he still grieved for our unborn children, but I didn't. I asked God to forgive us and to give us peace. I guess Brenton has to ask God for that on his own.

"God is going to bless us with more babies when the time is right."

I kissed his forehead and hopped off the counter.

***

I walked into the firm with my head held high. My Aldo pumps clicked against the hardwood as I walked into my office. I couldn't believe I had an office. There were two dozen roses on my desk and a card.

"You are the rose that grew from the concrete. Love Dad."

I smiled from ear to ear. I walked every inch of my tiny office. I opened the blinds, and to my surprise, I had a beautiful view of a flower garden. The firm was located on Cedar Road in Chesapeake, next to all of the city buildings. The landscaping in the area was breathtaking. I guess that was a perk of working so closely with city officials.

"Welcome, Sharae."

I turned around as I heard my name. *Oh my gosh! Who in the world is this fine-ass man*? His locs were neatly pinned up into a low bun. His suit looked to be of a brand I only saw in magazines, and his cologne could be smelled from the door.

"Hi, and you are?" I extended my hand toward the gentleman.

"Oh, excuse me, I'm Jamal, but people call me Lucky."

Lucky and I shook hands.

"Nice to meet you. May I ask why you're called Lucky?"

"Of course, my dad started this firm, and I've been the number one agent since I started four years ago. I am only 22 years old and a millionaire. I only close million-dollar deals."

I didn't take it as Lucky was bragging, just confident in who he is and what he has accomplished.

"Impressive!" That's all I could muster up to say.

"Maybe you can assist me with some of my clients ."

"I'd like that, Lucky, thanks."

Lucky left my office, and for some reason, I had an instant tingling between my legs. I've only felt this for Brenton, and it felt scary but good. I sat at my desk and daydreamed about Lucky. I imagined myself sitting on his lap with my skirt up to my waist. He gently kissed my neck and used his index finger to moisten my kitty. I took his finger and placed it in my mouth. I loved how it tasted. My love for mangoes and pineapples was evident.

There was a knock on my door, and I came

back to reality.

"Hey, Renee."

"Hey, Sharae, come with me, girl. Let's go look at your first property."

I eagerly followed behind Renee to her X6. Her SUV looked to be freshly washed and waxed.

"Rule #1: Always look the part, from your attire down to your vehicle."

Renee gave me advice without hesitation, and I soaked it all in. I looked at her manicured nails and how the red was slightly showing on the bottom of her shoe as she took each step. She wore a small Figaro chain with a J charm. I assumed the J was for her last name, Johnson.

Renee was my dad's age, but she could easily pass for a thirty-year-old. Renee has been an agent for 20 years, and it has provided her with a lucrative lifestyle. Renee's physical appearance was nothing like my mother's, but her confidence reminded me of her. While I was being mentored by Renee, I found myself imagining that she was my mother, and we were going to become this dynamic mother-daughter real estate duo. I was determined to be as successful as Renee, and I knew that with her and Lucky on my side, I couldn't lose.

***

Brenton and I arrived home at the same time. Brenton's energy didn't seem as bubbly as mine. His eyes suggested that he was drained.

"Hey baby, how was your day?" Brenton

kissed my forehead before he opened the front door for me.

"My day was amazing. I made the right choice as an agent. How was your day?"

"Long, to say the least. Elderly people are great to be around, but they're heavy, and some of them smell. And the aides are never anywhere to be found. I want to quit."

Brenton poured out his heart, and I instantly felt for him.

"Have a seat, sweetheart."

I decided not to tell Brenton how amazing my day was and that I had an offer in for my first listing; instead, I catered to him. I was too tired to cook, so I ordered salmon salads from a local restaurant. I made sure the bath water was the perfect temperature and lit the tealight candles that I had gotten from Dollar Tree a few weeks ago. Brenton wasn't really into slow jams, so I decided to put in his Tupac CD. I washed Brenton's body as Tupac bellowed about how some things would never change through the speakers. We didn't say any words, but I listened to his heart.

Over dinner, I told Brenton to quit his job. He disagreed and told me that he was the financial provider. There was no need for me to argue with Brenton over this. We both agreed that he would be the financial provider. My dad instilled in me as a little girl that a woman was free to obtain the lifestyle she desired and pursue any career, but that her income shouldn't be considered for bills. I am sure that thought process is why my mom was okay with letting her doctorate be only used as a display and happily lived as a full-time wife and mother.

5

Lucky had kept his word and allowed me to assist him on his million-dollar deals. In only six months as an agent, I had already made over six figures. The company's Christmas party was one that I had only seen on television. Everyone was dressed to perfection. I splurged on Brenton and me, buying us red bottoms and tailored clothes. Lucky introduced me to his tailoring guy, and things worked out perfectly.

"Babe, this is Lucky. Lucky, this is my boyfriend, Brenton."

The guys shook hands intensely, not taking their eyes off of one another. Brenton and Lucky chatted, and I decided to walk the room to get to know the spouses or significant others of my partners.

"Can I have everyone's attention?" A taller, older, darker version of Lucky stood at the center of the room.

"I'd like to welcome you all to Carter's Real Estate Firm's Annual Christmas Party. We have had the honor of being the number one firm not just in the Chesapeake area but in all of Virginia for the past 4 years."

Everyone began to clap and clink glasses at the news. I gleaned from ear to ear, soaking in being a part of such a successful company so young and so soon. I thought back to Lucky, who has only been with the company for four years. I guess it's safe to say that Lucky has a lot to do with the firm's success, and his alias was well deserved.

Mr. Carter asked all of the new agents to come forward. I walked to the middle of the room alongside Jack. Jack started at the firm a month before me but hasn't had as much success as me. He had a great mentor, but he wasn't eager to close deals. The rumor is that Jack was a trust fund kid, and he only chose real estate so that his parents wouldn't hound him about having a job. He barely came to the office three times per week.

Mr. Carter stood in between us, and his cologne was breathtaking. He wasn't fine like Lucky, but he damn sure was handsome. He wore his hair in locs as well. It must've been a family thing because later that evening I met Mrs. Carter, Lucky's mother, and she also wore her hair in locs, which was more stylish, of course.

Mrs. Carter seemed like a great southern woman. I learned that she was an underwriter and inspired the family's business. Before I could introduce Mrs. Carter to Brenton, she hinted at

Jamal and me going on a date. I like that she referred to her son by his birth name.

"Mrs. Carter, this is my boyfriend, Brenton. We grew up together."

"Only your boyfriend. So, Brenton, why haven't you made an honest woman of Sharae? From what I've heard, she's the total package."

I didn't expect that. Had Lucky told her about me or had Mr. Carter told her about my work ethic? Either way I blushed and started to sweat under my arms.

Brenton responded confidently, informing Mrs. Carter that marriage was in our future and possibly children. I lowered my head when Brenton mentioned children. He didn't know that after the last abortion, I decided to get on birth control. There was no need for any more accidents. I started taking the pill. It seemed to have the fewest side effects. I did want to have children one day, but honestly, I was more enticed by money at this point in my life. I loved how my mom gave up her career for me, but I also loved how Renee was a career woman. When I become a mom, I want to have the luxury of staying home, and Brenton's income or drive couldn't provide that, at least not right now.

"Excuse me. I need to go to the ladies' room."

I went into the restroom to wipe under my arms and freshen my lipstick. As I exited the ladies' room, Lucky grabbed my arm and guided me into the coat room.

"Lucky, what are you doing?"

"What I've wanted to do for the past six months."

Before I could object, Lucky's tongue was down my throat. I didn't reject him. I did the opposite and matched his energy. A voice interrupted us, and we snuck out separately.

The car ride home was silent on my behalf, but Brenton was full of energy.

"Sharae, I love your firm. Everyone seems so nice. I have to admit, how you have talked about Lucky, I was initially intimidated, but after meeting him, I see that he is a man who is about his business, and helping you win helps him win."

My heart skipped a beat as Brenton spoke. Lucky was talking about his business, and after tonight, it seemed as if he wanted me to be a part of that business.

"Yeah, Lucky is cool, babe, no worries."

"I'm going to quit my job, Sharae. I didn't want you to know until I had more details, but Old Dominion University is looking for a physical therapist for their athletics department. The pay begins at a little under six figures, and if I'm good, I could eventually progress to a professional team. I interviewed last week, and I'm pretty much guaranteed the job."

"Yesssss Brenton! This is exciting. I am glad you are following your dreams."

Our night ended on a high note like it always did, but this time, as I made love to my boyfriend, I envisioned it being Lucky.

I pretended that I was running my fingers through his hair as he gave me the ride of my life. Brenton didn't know the difference. His goal from the beginning was to make sure I climaxed. He didn't care how I got there.

6

Life was happening so fast. It was the end of 2005. It seems like just yesterday I was walking across the stage to accept my high school diploma. Brenton and I went home to Florida for New Year's Eve. My dad insisted that we attend the watch night service at church. After we prayed our way into the New Year, it happened. Brenton got down on one knee in front of the sanctuary with both our families present and asked me to marry him.

As long as I could remember, I wanted to marry Brenton. Growing up, I would sign my name as Sharae Brothers. I even gave our imaginary children names, which all started with the letter B: Brice, Breon, and Belle. I thought three children would be perfect - two boys and one girl, my princess Jasmine.

"Sharae, say something!" Mimi nudged me as the congregation waited for my response.

"Yes, yes, yes! I'll marry you, Brenton."

Brenton picked me up and twirled me around. I gazed at the Tiffany diamond that had once been my mother's. I knew my dad was happy. He never said it, but I could always tell that he was concerned that I didn't know how to receive love. He would always tell me that I deserved love and that everyone wasn't going to leave me.

The next day, Mimi and I went to lunch to catch up. I hadn't seen her since high school graduation. We filled each other in on our lives. Mimi was doing well. She stayed in Daytona Beach and graduated from Bethune Cookman College with a degree in education. She worked as a 5th-grade teacher at the very place we met, Westside Elementary.

"I know you, Sharae, and with that being said, who has you distracted from your Prince Charming? As long as I could remember, it has always been Brenton and Sharae, but how you were in a daze last night, I can tell that you might have your eyes somewhere else."

"Was it that obvious?"

Mimi was right. All I could think about was Lucky.

"Damn, we really are besties. Well, there is this guy who just does something to me. Besides the fact that he is fine as hell, he's smart, not just academically. He knows how to move in all types of rooms and talk to anyone. Everyone calls him Lucky, but I prefer to call him by the name his mother gave him: Jamal. Jamal means beauty, and that man is beautiful."

"Girl, you got me over here visualizing the Prince of Zamunda."

Mimi and I both laughed.

I hadn't been alone with Lucky since our kiss. Not that I didn't have the opportunity, but I was afraid to act on what my body was calling me to do. I loved Brenton, but it's like the spark is gone in our relationship. The sex was still A1, but there was no dreaming. I like to think that we, as humans, can dream while we are awake. We can believe that there are great things in this world for us, and we have to go after them. Brenton was practical. Although he decided to go towards his big goal of being a physical therapist for a sports team, in my eyes, he was still playing it safe.

Mimi ended our lunch date. She had another date with the principal of Westside Elementary - yes, her boss. He was married, but Mimi insisted that he loved her more than he loved his wife. I didn't want to be the one to tell her that this 40-year-old man was never going to leave his wife of 10 years just because she gave him amazing sex. Mimi was definitely dreaming. She told me all about the sex they had in her classroom or his office. I laughed at her telling me how one of her students found a condom wrapper by her desk, and she blamed it on the students. At least she was safe.

Before heading back to Virginia, Brenton and I stopped on the avenue and got some wings from Bethune Grill. There were no other wings that could compare. The avenue was packed as always. The line at Bethune Grill was out the door, and the car wash across the street was flooded. I missed Daytona. It was just enough, but not too hood for me.

Brenton and I saw a few of our classmates. Some looked good, and some looked like they were slowly letting the idea of being mediocre settle in. I could tell that *ecstasy* and *flakka* were making their way through my hometown. Quite a few people were beginning to look like rock monsters. That's what we called crackheads in the south. Over lunch. Mimi told me only about the people who were doing well. I respected her for that. We've never been fans of talking negatively about other people, not even in high school.

***

Brenton and I made it back to Virginia. The year 2006 was off to a wonderful start. Brenton accepted the job at Old Dominion University, and Lucky invited me to follow him to The Carter 2.0. The Carter family decided it was well overdue for the family to branch out to another location and give more access to the high-profile Virginia Beach clients. I accepted the offer. I overheard Lucky and Renee talking as I packed up my office.

"Lucky, be careful with her. You two may not want the same things."

"Thanks, Ms. Renee, for the advice, but you know that I always get what I want, and what I want is Sharae."

My heart skipped a beat as I heard my name. I was instantly turned on by Jamal's aggressive yet sultry tone. Another woman who had a good man and who was planning a wedding would have run from Jamal, but I did the total opposite. I picked up the box off of my desk and smiled as I thought about what Jamal was willing to do to win me.

***

"Sharae, have you decided on a wedding date?"

Brenton placed his arms around my waist as I cooked dinner. I made his favorites: fried chicken, mashed potatoes, and asparagus. He is such a simple man.

"I was thinking we should get married on New Year's Day 2007. It's a year from the proposal and will give you time to get settled into your new position."

"That's why I love you, babe. Always thinking of me."

Brenton was right. I was always thinking of him, but now I'm ready to think of myself.

Brenton and I ate dinner and talked about the wedding and the possibility of buying a home. We could afford a home now, but I wasn't sure that I was ready to take this step with him.

I lay on Brenton's chest as he watched Samuel L. Jackson play a Joe Clark role in the movie Coach Carter. I guess I dozed off because I woke up to my cell phone buzzing. It was Jamal.

"Hey Lucky, what's going on?"

"There's this property in the Hickory area of Chesapeake that I want you to see. Are you available now?"

"Lucky, it's already 8:00 p.m. Can it wait until tomorrow?" Brenton watched me as I talked on the phone.

"Not really, but if you don't want the commission, I understand."

"No, I do. Let me chat with Brenton. Text me the address."

I hung up the phone, and before I could speak, Brenton assured me that I should go meet with Lucky.

I arrived at the house an hour later, and it was gorgeous. I looked in the yard for a for sale sign, but there wasn't one. I guess it hasn't officially been placed on the market yet. The house was staged perfectly, almost as if I had decorated it.

"Hey, Jamal, what's so special about this house that I had to see it tonight?"

He grabbed my hand and led me into the master bedroom. The carpet was plush, and the bed was a California King covered with a white goose-down comforter swallowed in pillows. I went into the bathroom and was taken away by the vintage look. I looked down at the counter, and there was a blue box. Jamal snuck up behind me and grabbed my left hand. He slowly removed the engagement ring that Brenton had placed there on New Year's Day. There were no words.

Jamal opened the box, and there was a two-carat pear-shaped diamond ring. He placed it on my finger. I turned towards Jamal, and tears began to fill my eyes.

"I can't do this. I'm marrying Brenton. I'm supposed to marry Brenton."

Jamal didn't speak. He picked me up and carried me to the bed. Jamal undressed me. I sat patiently as he removed his clothes. Jamal was beautiful everywhere. Still no words.

Jamal used his tongue to explore my body. He started with my toes, making his way up my calf, then spread my thighs, and stopped at Miss Kitty. His tongue was powerful yet relaxing. I felt comfortable, like I was supposed to be here.

"Put it in."

I lifted Jamal's head to look into his eyes. Still no words. He lowered his head and continued to devour me. I lost count after I climaxed the third time. If I were truly a meal, he would've cleaned his plate.

After what seemed like an eternity, Jamal went into the bathroom. He came back with a warm washcloth and began to wash Miss Kitty. Brenton has never washed me. He never even brought me a towel after our sessions. Jamal put his clothes back on, and I started to become confused.

"You aren't going to let me feel you? Don't you want to feel me?"

"Sharae, when you're ready, this is your home. And when you're ready, we'll feel one another, but until then, we'll remember this moment."

I got dressed, and Jamal led me to the door. I faced him, and he gave me a simple forehead kiss.

Brenton was asleep when I arrived home. I showered and snuggled behind him. He was snoring lightly. I felt guilty for allowing Jamal to taste me, but not guilty enough to not want it to happen again.

I fell asleep smiling, thinking that I was the lucky one. I was in such a deep sleep that I didn't hear Brenton get out of bed. He was enjoying his new job and never missed a morning run. Miss Kitty was feening for penetration after last night's tease. I could've waited on Brenton, but instead, I decided to take care of myself. My panties got caught on my ring as I slid them down. *Oh shit*! I never replaced my ring with Jamal's! *Fuck*! I heard Brenton coming in the door, and I jumped up. I threw Jamal's ring into my purse just as Brenton made his way into our bedroom.

Brenton greeted me with a kiss.

"Good morning, sweet thing. You must've had some good dreams last night. You were smiling and moaning all night."

"I don't remember, babe, but I'm sure I was dreaming of you."

I kissed Brenton's neck, hiding my face from the guilt that I felt. I did have good dreams last night, but they were all Jamal. Seeing Jamal's manhood let me know that he wasn't as well-endowed as

Brenton, but honestly, I didn't need a Mandingo warrior. I only needed to be taken care of.

"Sharae, where's your ring?"

I was caught off guard by the question. I stuttered but managed to tell Brenton that I had taken the ring to be sized down. It was a nice fit, but I would like it to be a little more snug. Brenton didn't question it.

"Next weekend is my mother's 50th birthday, and I was thinking we should go home for the weekend. What do you think?"

"I wish I could, babe, but Carter 2.0 is hosting our grand opening. Because Jamal and I are the heads of the firm, I have to be there."

"Who is Jamal?"

"Lucky is Jamal. I prefer to call him by his birth name. It's more professional."

Brenton gave me a side eye, but again, he didn't question my response.

"I'll be sure to send Mama Brothers a nice gift. You know your mama loves a nice gift."

I put a mental note in my head to get Mama Brothers a nice piece of jewelry for her birthday.

Brenton left for the day. My phone buzzed. It was a text message from Jamal.

"*I guess you made your decision,*" the message read, followed by a picture of my original engagement ring.

"Please bring my ring to the office. That ring belonged to my mother."

Jamal didn't reply. His silence was enticing.

It's like he knew when to use his words.

The following Friday, I dropped Brenton off at the airport for his flight home. I had gotten Mama Brothers a gold Movado watch. I knew she would love it.

The grand opening was a total success. Having a team makes things so easy. We welcomed two new agents to the team, husband-and-wife duo Kelly and Michael Anderson. They've been agents for only two years, but they hit the ground running and wanted to grow with a black-owned company. It seems like everyone was trying to be on the pro-black and gay gravy train. It was almost like a trend. Jamal and I both agreed that having some white faces in Virginia Beach could be beneficial to Carter 2.0.

After the grand opening, Jamal asked me to take him to pick up his car from the dealership, where it was being serviced. We pulled up to the BMW dealership on Virginia Beach Blvd. I followed Jamal inside. Once we got to the counter, the associate asked if I was Ms. Smith with a smile.

"Yes, I am Sharae Smith," I answered.

She handed me a set of keys.

"You're one lucky girl."

"Jamal, what's going on?"

"You can't represent Carter 2.0 and keep driving that Honda Civic."

I loved my little Honda Civic, but it was a little girl's car. Jamal led me to a black-on-black 650i

BMW. The seats were red, and my name was engraved on the headrest.

"Jamal, I can't accept this car. You can't buy me a car. I have a fiancé."

"You have two fiancés, Sharae, but only one has bought you a house and a car."

Why did he make everything sound so easy? Jamal is showing up in ways that every girl would dream of.

I got into the car and drove away. I could afford the car, but I didn't discuss it with Brenton. How was I going to explain this?

I found myself driving to the property in Hickory. I sat in front of the house. I didn't have a key, so I couldn't go in. I called Jamal.

"Come home."

Twenty minutes later Jamal pulled into the driveway behind me. I followed him into the house. Everything was just as we had left it. Jamal ordered takeout. We stayed up all night talking about our childhoods, our dreams, and our future. I wanted to be with Jamal, but I didn't want to hurt Brenton, and I didn't want to disappoint my dad. My dad felt that I was safe with Brenton.

"Jamal, what if I am not the woman that you think that I am? What if I don't measure up to the wife that you desire?"

"From the day I first saw you, I knew that you were the one. I've never withheld myself from sex. I've been abstinent since I laid eyes on you. I want you, and only you. I want you to be my wife and have my children."

I hadn't told Jamal that I had previously had abortions. We talked about everything, but that was something I wanted to keep to myself.

We spent all weekend together. Saturday was filled with shopping at McArthur Mall, and Sunday we went to a popular church on Military Highway. I had never been to a megachurch. It seemed like a movie premiere or something. Mr. and Mrs. Carter attended the same church, and we had lunch afterward.

"So, Sharae, how is your boyfriend? What's his name, Brandon?" Mrs. Carter asked.

"His name is Brenton, and he's doing great. He's visiting family in Florida."

"What are you doing here with my son?"

"Mom, chill," Jamal interjected as Mrs. Carter grilled me.

"I'm here because Jamal invited me to church. We're friends."

"Look, call it what you want, but don't lead my son on. He's a loverboy, and he has his mind set on you. You're a good girl, but no one is worthy of breaking my son's heart."

I listened to Mrs. Carter, and she was right. I didn't want to break her son's heart. I didn't want to break anyone's heart.

"I won't."

***

It was time for me to pick up Brenton from

the airport. I parked curbside and waited for my prince charming. I was still dressed in my church clothes.

"Whoa, baby, did you rent this car?" Brenton asked as he placed his bags in the trunk.

"Nope, it's the company's car. They want us to look like money while we close deals." I remembered what Renee had told me.

"That's cool and all, but why is your name on the headrest?"

"That was an add-on that I paid for myself. After two years with the company, it's officially mine."

The lies rolled off of my tongue, and my stomach fluttered.

I listened as Brenton told me about his mother's party and how she loved the watch. I was happy to have my fiancé home. I missed him even though I did spend the entire time with Jamal.

7

The next few months seemed to fly by. It was July, and my birthday was only 15 days away. I hadn't decided on any plans, but I knew I wanted my 23rd birthday to be fun. Real estate came with a big payout, but there was a lot of hard work, and I was ready to relax.

Although Jamal had not made any more sexual advances towards me, he didn't hesitate to have flowers delivered to my office, pay for my lunch, or have random pieces of jewelry and perfume waiting on my desk. My latest gift was a diamond tennis bracelet - not a diamond-cut bracelet, but a 3-carat diamond bracelet. After the diamond studs I came home flaunting, I knew better than to bring any more of my gifts home. Brenton asked to see the receipt for the earrings, and when I couldn't produce it, he insinuated that I was having sex with Jamal. We had our first real argument, and he stayed out all night. The next day, he returned home as if nothing had happened.

I attempted to redeem myself by giving

Brenton mind-blowing oral, but he brushed me off. For a second, I thought that he may have cheated on me, but then I remembered that this was Brenton. He has loved me since before I had a menstrual cycle. The thought quickly left my head.

It was Sunday morning, and I decided to take the day off. I worked so much, almost seven days a week, so I decided to dedicate at least one day a month to Brenton and me. We lay in bed and watched cartoons.

"Babe let's go to Jamaica for your birthday. Invite Mimi and whoever her lover is, and I'll invite my coworker Samone and her boyfriend."

I hadn't met Samone yet, but Brenton always included her in the debriefing of his day. She seemed to show him the ropes at ODU and help him get acclimated. I guess they had become friends because he wanted to invite her on MY birthday trip.

"Why would we invite Samone?"

"She's a cool person, and her boyfriend seems to be, too."

"When did you meet her boyfriend?"

"I crashed at their house the night that you and I had that big fight over Lucky."

Instantly, I felt guilty, even though I wasn't sleeping with Jamal. I agreed to his idea to take the trip to Jamaica and invite others.

Brenton immediately texted Samone the idea, and within minutes she was all for the trip. She didn't even discuss it with her boyfriend. I didn't let

Brenton know that was a little suspicious. I just put the thought in the back of my mind.

The night before our trip to Jamaica, Samone's boyfriend broke his ankle and couldn't go on the trip. We all flew out of Norfolk International and met Mimi and her boss in Jamaica. To my surprise, the principal had left his wife for Mimi, at least for the next five days.

Samone kept saying how she felt like she was a third wheel, and Mimi didn't hesitate to agree with her. There was no denying that Samone was attractive according to any man's standards. Her skin was deep chocolate, her hair was bone straight, like she had Indian in her blood (direct lineage, not a second cousin twice removed), and she had dimples that reminded you of the actress Lauren London. You could tell that Samone was an athletic trainer. Her body was tight and loose in all the right places.

Brenton had become jealous of Jamal and I's relationship, although we didn't have a relationship outside of work. Jamal relaxed on his advances towards me, but Brenton said he could tell that Lucky was in love with me, and he wasn't sure what I felt for him. I wasn't in love with Jamal, but I was intrigued by him.

"Hey, Sharae, who does your hair?" Samone asked as we sat at the edge of the infinity pool.

"I usually do it myself. You would think after almost five years in Virginia I would have a hairstylist."

"If you ever get tired of doing it yourself, I work in a salon on Saturdays, and I don't want to brag, but I am a beast when it comes to natural hair."

"Thanks, Samone. I'll take you up on that offer. It's time I start shopping around for a hairstylist for the wedding."

Mimi splashed water on me, and I jumped in the pool, chasing behind my friend. Everyone joined, and we started up a game of Marco Polo. It was Brenton's turn as Marco. We all swam around the pool, yelling "Polo" as he searched for us.

Brenton seemed drawn to Samone's voice. He came up behind her and grabbed her waist. She giggled, he giggled, and I felt uneasy. There was a spark between them. Mimi's boss could feel the tension and suggested we all take a shot of tequila at the poolside bar. One shot turned into two, and then, I think, four. I don't remember much except for Brenton carrying me to our suite.

There was a knock on our door. Brenton was sleeping. I looked through the peephole and saw Samone. She was holding some headache medicine and ginger ale. I opened the door.

"Hey girl, what's up?" I asked Samone as I peeked at the wall clock. It read 3:16 a.m.

"I couldn't sleep, so I wanted to check on you."

She handed me the medicine along with the drink and walked into the suite.

"Thanks. Have a seat. Brenton is sleeping."

Samone followed me to the couch in the sitting area and sat next to me. I felt a little awkward because I thought of how she looked at Brenton earlier and wasn't sure if I should check her now or give her a chance to check herself.

"I know it's weird that I'm here and Keith isn't. Keith is my boyfriend, by the way. But I want you to know I wouldn't have come if Brenton didn't insist on our meeting."

"Samone, are you fucking Brenton?"

"What?! Sharae, no! I would never, well, unless..." Samone's voice drifted.

"Unless what?" I asked directly.

"Unless I could have you also."

Samone moved in closer to me, and I could feel her breath on my lips. My mind told me to scoot away, but my body froze.

Samone began to lick my lips as she whispered the word *relax*. I began to relax, and I started to caress Samone's breast. She was a perky C-cup. Samone and I slid down to the floor. I guess Brenton had helped me into a nightshirt earlier. She lifted it over my head. Samone stared at my body. I had never even thought of experiencing sex with a woman, but nothing felt strange about what was happening.

"Brenton told me your body was amazing, but this is more than I expected."

I didn't say a word. I only wondered what type of conversations Brenton and Samone had about me.

Samone was gentle with me, just as Jamal was. She took two fingers and slid them in and out of Miss Kitty. Next, she straddled me in a scissoring position and thrust her vagina into mine. I matched her strokes until she climaxed. She squirted all over me. It felt amazing. When I opened my eyes, Brenton was standing over us, naked. He didn't say a word. I felt embarrassed.

Brenton got down on his knees and placed his penis in Samone's mouth. She sucked him slowly. I watched. Brenton exploded, and Samone swallowed every drop of him.

"Both of you bend over on your knees," Brenton instructed Samone and me, and we did as he said.

Brenton took turns entering Samone and me slowly, yet aggressively. We both climaxed, and Brenton also allowed his semen to pour over both of our backs. We all climbed into bed and fell asleep.

"Happy Birthday, baby!" Brenton woke me up with a forehead kiss and a waffle with a candle. Samone was wrapped in a towel and sat at the edge of the bed.

"Have y'all fucked before?" I asked Samone and Brenton.

Brenton responded, "No. We have flirted, but I told Samone I would never cheat on you, and she never pressed the issue."

"Brenton always talks about you, Sharae. He

adores you. I am bisexual, and I wanted to know why he was so in love with you. As much as he talked about you, I felt like I knew you. Your work ethic reminds me of myself, and once I saw your body at the pool, I understood why he views you as the total package. I agree with him. You didn't disappoint."

"I'm flattered, Samone, but I'm not bisexual. I've never been with a woman before you."

"Would you be with me again?"

Surprisingly, I responded, "Yes."

"Brenton, what are you feeling?" I asked as he sat quietly.

"I am feeling great, honestly. I love you, Sharae. I'm in love with you, and I want you to be my wife, as you already know. I also enjoyed last night and wouldn't mind us having fun from time to time."

"So, you want both of us?"

"I would like to have sex with both of you, yes."

No way am I welcoming my 23rd birthday in a polygamous relationship that can't be real. My mind was racing. What does this even mean? I don't want to date a woman.

"I don't want to date you, Samone."

"I don't want to date you either, Sharae, but I do want to fuck you. Can we do that?"

Samone crawled towards me on the bed and sat her vagina on my face. I had no idea what to do, but I did what I knew felt good to me. I licked her until she slid on top of me. Samone kissed me and twirled her fingers in my hair.

"Happy Birthday, friend."

The rest of my birthday trip was adventurous. Dunn's River Falls was my favorite excursion. Mimi and her boss were seemingly inseparable, and Samone no longer felt like a third wheel. I made up my mind that my new sex life would be left in Jamaica. Yes, I had fun with Samone, but this isn't something I wanted to do regularly, and I knew that God was watching. I have to save my sins for bigger things.

Still Adulting

8

Another Monday morning. Brenton got up excited for work and took his morning run. I still hadn't figured out the coffee thing, so I made tea instead. I read somewhere that green tea gets you going just as coffee does without the crash.

When Brenton returned, we ate breakfast together and sipped our tea. We were in a good place. We hadn't discussed Jamaica much, but he reassured me that whatever I wanted to do with or without Samone, he would respect me.

I couldn't wait to get to the office. Work is the one place I felt as if I was in total control, and I couldn't wait to see Jamal.

***

Jamal tapped on my office door.

"Good morning, gorgeous. You were missed last week. How was your birthday?"

"Thanks, Jamal. My birthday was definitely not what I expected, but great."

"Well, tell me more about this unexpected birthday."

Jamal sat in the chair on the other side of my desk.

"I am not ready for that conversation yet, Jamal. I might not ever be."

"Whenever you are, I'm willing to listen. Oh, by the way, here's your birthday gift. I know you're a true Florida girl, so I got you these."

Jamal handed me two VIP tickets to see Trina in concert this Saturday night at the Amphitheater in Virginia Beach.

"Awww, thanks, Jamal. But who will I take? Are you into Trina?"

"Not particularly. I was thinking you could take one of your girlfriends if Brenton doesn't want to go."

"He'll listen to Trina, but he's not going to see her in concert."

My mind went to Samone. Just because I didn't want to sleep with her doesn't mean we can't hang out.

The day went smoothly. I hosted an open house for a property in Virginia Beach and gained some prospective clients.

Later that night, I asked Brenton if he would mind if I asked Samone to accompany me to the concert, and he was all for it. He gave me Samone's number, and before I knew it, we had a date to see the Baddest Bitch, Trina.

***

The work week always flew by because real

estate never stopped. At Carter 2.0, we only deal with pre-approved clients so that our time isn't wasted. Some realtors will hold prospective clients' hands and help them through the beginning phases of buying a home, but that's not us.

The Anderson's were closing deals left and right. They breathed real estate and had no desire to have children. Kelly told me that both she and Michael were only children and didn't like it. She said she couldn't see herself mothering more than one child, so they both decided on having none. I loved them for being firm. No one ever had to leave early because of children. I still wanted to have children, maybe in seven more years.

On Fridays, Jamal and I always have lunch together to catch up on the work week. Jamal usually introduces me to some fancy new restaurant, but not this week. We met at a small mom-and-pop restaurant in Portsmouth. I liked the atmosphere. It reminded me of home. I was still very much attracted to Jamal, but his advances had come to a halt. I was glad in a way, but unsure as to why.

"Are you ready for the concert?"

"Yes, sir, I have my booty shorts waiting," I laughed as I thought about me shaking my ass at Trina's concert.

Somehow I ended up telling Jamal all about Jamaica and Samone. I couldn't tell how Jamal felt regarding his facial expressions.

"So, you're okay with sharing your man? That doesn't seem like you, Sharae."

"I didn't think that I was, but once it was happening, I wasn't opposed to it."

"Would you share me?" Jamal leaned back in his chair and sipped his Jack and Coke.

"I guess we'd never know. Now would we, Jamal?"

"That's up to you. You still have a home to come to. I'm a man like most men, but if you were my fiancé, I wouldn't position you for something like that to even possibly happen. It sounds to me that Brenton and Samone set you up."

I didn't think that Brenton and Samone plotted that night in Jamaica, but then again, if Brenton wanted to openly be with another woman, what other way would he do it?

"I don't know about that, Jamal. Samone's boyfriend was supposed to be there also."

"See it your way, but drunk or not, Jamaica or not, I'd never be with another woman sexually if you were mine."

I was becoming turned on by Jamal's certainty that I was all he needed. He wasn't wrong. Why would Brenton have sex with Samone?

"Jamal, I'm ready for you to have me."

"As my wife?"

"Not technically, but I am ready to care for you and take care of you. Are you still celibate?"

"I am very much celibate, but I'm not ready to be thrown into your love triangle. If I make love to you, you'll be more confused. I need someone

76

sure about us."

Jamal always made so much sense. His patience has kept my panties moist. I'm not sure if I want to marry Brenton. I love him, but I'm not in love with him. I would never share a man I'm in love with.

Jamal and I finished lunch, and I followed him to our home. Jamal wanted to show me the backyard. He added a jacuzzi and deck. The landscaping was breathtaking. Red rose bushes filled every corner. I stood on the deck and exhaled. Jamal came up behind me and placed his hands on my shoulders. I could smell his Chanel cologne. It was a faint smell, but noticeable. He kissed my neck and led me to the patio furniture. I sat on his lap and allowed him to play with Miss Kitty. He was quickly aroused.

"Jamal, let me take care of you."

Jamal didn't say a word. He never said a word when we were intimate. After 30 minutes and climaxing three times, my phone rang. It was Samone.

"Hey, Samone."

"Hey girl, I was thinking Keith and Brenton could hang out while we're at the concert tomorrow. How about we meet at my house and leave from there? The guys can stay there or do whatever."

I agreed with Samone and hung up. Jamal was listening to our conversation.

"Look, Sharae, don't be naive with this situation."

"I'm not green, Jamal. Don't worry about me."

Saturday came, and we met up at Samone and Keith's home. They lived in a nice townhome in Virginia Beach, off of Independence Blvd., close to the Amphitheater. I was surprised when I met Keith to see that he was a white guy. I have no problem with interracial relationships, but Samone didn't take me as a woman who dated outside of her race. Keith didn't come off as a black or white guy. He looked like he wore shorts with long sleeves in December. Your typical white guy. His curly, dirty blonde hair reminded me of the actor Matthew McConaughey.

Keith and Brenton hit it off well, both sharing their interest in Marvel Comics and Tupac. Samone and I left for a night of partying. Trina was amazing, and when she called all her Florida girls to the stage, I couldn't resist.

I rapped along to every word and shook my ass like it was for sale. Samone and I laughed the entire ride home. I looked to my left, and Samone started smoking a joint. I had never smoked weed; in fact, I had never even tried it. She passed it to me and told me to inhale. I did, followed up by a lot of coughing and choking. Samone smiled. After a few pulls, I got used to it. I like how it made me feel.

We pulled back up to Samone's home around midnight. Keith and Brenton were at the kitchen table, playing cards. I sat on Brenton's lap and grinned.

"Samone, what did you give my girl? Why is she so giddy?"

"Nothing to worry about, Brenton, just something from God's garden."

Samone turned on some music, and the party continued in their living room. The shots started to get passed around, and Keith sparked up a joint. We were all drinking and smoking. Brenton didn't smoke. Samone began to dance seductively in front of Keith. She took off her top and exposed her braless chocolate breast. No one flinched, not even Keith. Samone moved to Brenton and pushed her boobs into his face. Brenton licked them. I just sat there. Keith moved next to me and asked me if I was okay. I didn't respond. He told me not to worry, and this is how they party. He handed me the joint. I smoked it. Keith pulled his shorts down and stood in front of me. He wasn't wearing any boxers, and his manhood went against every rumor I had heard about white men, except that it was pink. I looked at Brenton, and he had Samone bent over the chair as if she were someone he was familiar with. The only man I've been with sexually is Brenton, and as much as I craved Jamal, I knew that I was worth more than casual penetration.

"Keith, I'm sorry, but I'm not into casual sex."

Keith pulled up his shorts and mouthed, "Me either."

Samone and Brenton were oblivious to Keith and me. Samone began to yell Brenton's name, and

Brenton moaned loudly as he slumped his body over.

The car ride home was silent. Brenton placed his right hand on my knee as we drove back to Norfolk. I was apprehensive of Brenton's touch. I couldn't help but think to myself that all of this was my fault. This is my karma for not stopping Jamal's advances.

On Sunday morning, Brenton and I lay in bed together, watching reruns of Martin. The episode playing was the one when the character Pam was going to marry the rich man Simon, but she didn't because she found out he had multiple wives. I started to wonder if Brenton wanted multiple wives.

"Brenton, are you interested in polygamy, 'cause I'm not? I don't feel comfortable with what is happening in our sex lives."

"Sharae, chill out. Nothing is happening that you don't want to happen. You willingly had sex with Samone, just like you willingly flirt with Lucky, Jamal, or whatever his fucking name is."

Brenton began to raise his voice, but I wasn't moved by his anger.

"Think what you want to think, Brenton, but I know that you had sex with another woman. I was there, remember, or were you in so deep that you forgot I was there last night?"

"I was definitely in deep," Brenton said sarcastically, placing his hands behind his head.

I sat up and looked directly into Brenton's

eyes. He wasn't the boy that I fell in love with seven years ago when I gave him my precious gift. His eyes were cold. They pierced my heart. I was no longer his favorite girl. Samone gave Brenton something that he had only experienced with me, and he liked hers better.

"Brenton, we are less than six months away from our wedding. I don't want to go into it with infidelity."

"It's only infidelity if you don't accept it."

"What about God? What about our values and morals?"

"Look, we aren't little kids sneaking kisses. We are adults who like to have casual sex. I still love you and want to marry you. You weren't thinking about God when you were murdering our babies."

My heart sank. I couldn't swallow. Brenton resented me for having the abortions. *Say something, Sharae. Say something.*

"Brenton, fuck you!"

That's all I can muster up. I was hurt. I jumped out of bed, threw on my Baby Phat dress, and grabbed my car keys. I hopped on I64 with no destination in mind.

"Mommy, I need you. What is happening in my life? I know at 23 I should have fun, but does that mean degrading myself? I let God down. I let you down. I let Dad down. I let myself down."

Tears flowed from my eyes as I cried out to my mommy. I know she couldn't hear me, but I needed to tell someone. I drove back to the apartment I shared with Brenton, although my body told me to drive to the home I shared with Jamal. I didn't want to be a hypocrite. Brenton was hanging up the phone as I opened the front door.

"Hey Sharae."

Brenton stood up and met me in the middle of our living room. He grabbed my shoulders and looked into my eyes.

"I'm sorry."

Tears began to well up in Brenton's eyes. I believed him.

"I talked to your dad and told him everything."

"Why would you do that?"

"Because we need help. I am hurt by our babies. I'm jealous of your friendship with Lucky. I only used Samone because she was making me feel better. I don't want her. Your dad suggested premarital counseling, and I think we should do it."

My mind was all over the place. I could hear Brenton's voice, but he seemed so distant. I didn't want my dad to look at me as anything except for his baby girl.

The day seemed to move slowly. I cleaned until I got a headache from the fumes. There was a knock on our door. To my surprise, my dad sent me two dozen roses and a note that read, *"I'll always love you, baby girl. Love, Daddy."*

No More High School Sweethearts

9

The rest of the summer was painful. Brenton and I started premarital counseling, and we decided on individual counseling as well. I soon learned that growing pains referred to more than physical growth.

"Jamal, I'm leaving for Florida tomorrow, and when I return, I'll be Mrs. Brothers. I'm sorry for leading you on these past six months. I pray that I haven't hurt you."

Jamal sat across from me, picking at his chicken Parmesan. The restaurant, Macaroni Grill, was his choice for our weekly meeting.

I remember the time I overheard Renee tell Brenton to be careful, and the other time his mother informed me not to hurt her son. Neither one of us had taken their advice.

"Jamal, say something."

"What do you want me to say, Sharae? Where are you two registered?"

Jamal had a sarcastic tone to his voice; one I hadn't heard before.

"So, after everything that happened last summer, you still want to marry this man? A man who was willing to allow you to sleep with another man just because he was hurt!"

I grabbed Jamal's right hand with my left. My mother's Tiffany ring was shining. I made sure to have it cleaned before the ceremony.

"Life isn't simple, Jamal. Brenton and I were meant to be, and I forgive him. I have to."

"You have to because you want to or because God wants you to."

"That's just it. My whole being is based on my relationship with God. A relationship I put to the side because I wasn't focused on God's plan."

Jamal loosened his hand from mine and leaned in towards me.

"Sharae, I know you. I've listened to you for hours about your childhood, about your goals, the love you have for your father, and how much you miss your mother. Through our countless conversations, you never told me, why not me?"

"It can't be you because there is Brenton. Maybe in another lifetime, but in this life I am destined to be Sharae Brothers."

I felt someone staring at me. I looked to my left, and there sat Samone and a guy who was not Keith. She walked over to our table with what looked like a baby bump.

"Hey Sharae, surprising to see you here. How's Brenton?"

"I'm just having a business meeting. No surprises. Samone, this is Lucky. Lucky, this is Samone."

I didn't want to call him Jamal in front of Samone - that was something special I shared with him. The two extended their arms for a handshake. Jamal gave a half-smile.

"Brenton is doing well. We both are."

Jamal quit his job at Old Dominion University a month prior and transferred to our alma mater, Norfolk State University. Our premarital counselor suggested that we both switch jobs, but Brenton insisted that I didn't leave Carter 2.0. He said he trusted me.

"Is that a baby bump, Samone?"

"It is," Samone responded casually with a sly grin on her face.

A lump formed in my throat. I swallowed hard.

"How far along are you?"

"A little over 20 weeks."

Samone rubbed her belly and walked away. I was in a daze.

"Sharae, are you okay?" Jamal asked with sincerity in his voice.

I shrugged my shoulders.

"It looks like you and Brenton will need to have a conversation."

Jamal was right, but we're two days away from our wedding. Do I even want to know if this is his baby? Do I want him to know?"

I told Jamal I would catch up with him later. Before I left Jamal's presence, he grabbed my hand. I stared into his eyes and listened as he told me that forgiveness does not mean forgetting. I let a simple tear roll down my cheek without responding to Jamal.

I decided I didn't want to go home, so I checked myself into a hotel along Virginia Beach's strip. Jack Frost was out, but there was something about me watching the waves crash from my balcony that was calming. I decided to give Brenton a call so that he wouldn't worry about me.

"Hey, Brenton."

"Hey, babe, where are you?"

"I'm at a hotel. I need to say something, so listen."

It sounded as if Brenton held his breath.

"I saw Samone today, and she's pregnant."

There was a long pause, and I could hear Brenton take a deep breath.

"I know."

"What do you mean, you know? How? When did you speak with her?"

"She called me two months ago and told me. She said she wasn't sure if the baby was mine or Keith's."

"You don't think this is something I need to know, Brenton? You were just going to marry me with a possible baby on the way? That is selfish!"

I hung up the phone and cried into my pillow.

Brenton and I had done so much healing through counseling, and for what? For me to become a stepmother? Hell no! I am not being a part of this baby's life!

I called my dad.

"Hey, Dad."

"Hey baby girl, what's ailing you? You sound upset."

I let out a scream. My dad didn't say a word. I told him about Samone's pregnancy.

"Baby girl, I love you and I love Brenton, but you are my child. You and Brenton made some selfish, worldly decisions that put you in this place. I am not happy about this news, but I want you to go to God before you make any hasty decisions."

"Dad, the wedding is off, at least until there is a paternity test."

"I understand, baby girl. I'll have Caprice send out emails to the guest and all of the companies involved."

"Thank you, Daddy. I'm sorry."

I felt relief knowing that my dad supported my decision. I am big on family, and there is no way I will willingly become a stepmother at 23 years old. I don't want to be anyone's mother right now.

I hit the next number that was in my recent call log.

"Come to this address."

Within 30 minutes, Jamal was knocking on my hotel room's door.

Jamal entered quietly. He was holding a bag

from Walgreens. I closed the door behind him. Jamal ran me a bath using a eucalyptus bubble bath he purchased. He also lit a lavender candle.

I sank into the tub. Jamal left me alone. I prayed, I cried, and I prayed some more. I didn't understand why God was allowing this to happen. Haven't I endured enough?

After about 45 minutes, Jamal came into the bathroom naked. He slipped into the bathtub behind me. I could feel his manhood against my back. He washed me. We sat in silence until the water turned cold.

I dried Jamal's body, and he dried mine. I wasn't interested in having sex with him and he didn't try to please me. I laid on his chest. I fell asleep to his heartbeat.

Jamal and I both must have been overdue to sleep in. We didn't wake up until 10:00 a.m. I had several missed calls from Brenton and over 30 text messages.

The last one read, *"Just let me know that you are alive."*

I texted back and told Brenton that I wanted to postpone the wedding and that I wouldn't be home until I was ready.

He replied, "Understandable."

I already planned to be away from work for the next two weeks. Jamal called the Andersons and asked them to hold down the firm for the next week while he took care of some family matters. Jamal asked me to accompany him to Hawaii. Without hesitation, I said yes.

Later that evening, with no luggage, we boarded a plane to Hawaii. Jamal informed me that his family owned a vacation home there. After our 10-hour flight, we landed in Honolulu. Carter's vacation home was immaculate. Every room was covered in white decor. The first night and day we stayed in, attempting to recover from jet lag. We picked up a few clothing items on our way from the airport. The house was equipped with the toiletries we needed. Jamal had groceries delivered and hired a chef and housekeeper for the week. I could get used to this.

On Tuesday, we went on a volcano tour. I learned that Jamal spent his summers here. He was a great tour guide. We ended the evening at a luau, where I won the limbo contest.

Jamal and I talked for hours every night. I learned that he had an older brother, Jameson. Jameson died in a secret deployment in 2000. He was a Marine and only 21 years old. This was the first time I saw Jamal cry. He went on to tell me that he planned to join the Marines as well. He wanted to be like his big brother, but his death took that dream from his heart. He also told me about Alex. She was his high school sweetheart but chose to go to prom instead of his brother's funeral with him. He never spoke to her again. He says he has seen her around Virginia, but in his eyes, she's dead to him. When he spoke of Alex, he was emotionless. I told Jamal about my abortions. I didn't cry. The week ended, and it was time to face the reality of my life.

Jamal and I walked to the airport's parking garage to retrieve our cars.

"So, Jamal, where does this lead us?"

Jamal opened my car door. I paused and looked him in the eyes.

"I love you. I have loved you since the first day I walked into your office, but I don't want to be the rebound guy. Take some time to focus on you, Sharae, and I promise when you're ready, I'll be here."

Jamal closed my car door and watched me drive away. The year 2007 didn't start as I had planned.

I drove to the apartment I shared with Brenton. I opened the door and was surprised by the smell of bacon frying and the artist Pharrell blasting through the speakers. The biggest surprise was seeing Samone come out of my kitchen.

"So, I guess we're just one big happy family?" Brenton was startled by my voice.

"Sharae, hey, I didn't know when you were coming back."

"And that's a reason to have another woman in our home?"

Samone didn't say a word. She stood frozen in a sports bra, showing her growing baby bump and black leggings. The baby was giving her skin an even more beautiful glow. She looked sunkissed. Her hair was up in a messy bun, with a few pieces dangling. She spoke on Brenton's behalf.

"Sharae, Brenton is just making sure his baby is okay. Men like to be a part of the process, but I guess you wouldn't know anything about that."

I assume that was a dagger, but what Samone didn't know is that when God forgave me, no devil in hell or on earth could condemn me.

"Samone, fuck you, your baby, and Brenton! Do you even know who the dad is, or are you just hoping it's a black man's baby? Get the fuck out of my house!"

Samone grabbed her coat and headed for the door. Brenton stood in the way of the door.

"Wait! Everyone, just calm down! Sharae, what if this is my baby? I can't let her go through this pregnancy alone. I want to be a father to my child."

"Brenton, you are a joke! You had sex with a whore and now have hopes of fathering a baby with her?!"

"She's doing what you didn't have the guts to do, Sharae!"

"Brenton, let's not forget that you took me to get the second abortion, so save the guilt trip for someone else."

I headed towards the bedroom to grab some clothes.

"Bye Brenton. I hope you have a happy ever after. Actually, I don't."

I headed towards the home that Jamal bought for us. I called Jamal on the way so that he could meet me at the house and let me in. Jamal arrived shortly after I did. He was wearing a gray Armani sweatsuit that was snug in all of the right places. His hair hung loosely down his back, and it was something about the way he walked with confidence that made me briefly forget about my drama. I followed Jamal into the house. He turned and handed me a set of keys.

"Sharae, this is your home. I bought it for us, but I'm not moving in here with you unless you are my wife. I know you aren't ready, and I am not rushing you. Take the time that you need."

I respected Jamal for respecting me. Jamal didn't stick around for too long. After he left, I did what most women do when they need a new start: online shopping. I went to my favorite work wardrobe website and ordered almost everything that came in a size 5. I wanted to be sexy for my next phase of life, so I went on the Arden B and BeBe website, where I found the best miniskirts and bodycon dresses. I was going to be a whole new woman once the spring season came.

I decided I would go to McArthur Mall the next day to get some shoes from Aldo. After charging over $3,000 on my AMEX, I felt lonely. I texted Brenton and asked him if he could box up all of my belongings, and I would pick everything up later this week. I went into the kitchen hoping some type of food would be there, but it wasn't. I ordered a pizza from Papa John's. I opted for pick-up so that

I could stop at Blockbuster's and rent a DVD.

I walked through the aisles of Blockbuster, hoping something would catch my attention. I bent down to grab the movie *Dreamgirls*. I'm sure I would be entertained by a movie that starred Beyoncé, Jamie Foxx, and Eddie Murphy.

There was a tap on my shoulder, and as I stood up, I recognized Keith. There he stood with a baseball cap covering his dirty blonde hair, a long-sleeved shirt that read UCLA, khaki shorts, and flip-flops. He was your typical white guy.

"Hey, Sharae."

"Hi, Keith."

Neither Keith nor I spoke for a moment, and then we both began to speak at the same time. Keith started to tell me how he asked Samone to get an abortion because of the uncertainty and that he was only staying in Virginia to find out if the baby was his. He doubted that it was his baby.

"Samone and I always wore condoms. She was adamant about it, but with Brenton, she had no regard. She's in love with him."

"I'm sorry, Keith. It seems like we are both caught up in a whirlwind."

"You aren't. You can walk away and never look back. You don't have to be a part of this."

"Is it that easy to walk away from someone who has loved you before you loved yourself? That you have shared almost everything that mattered with?"

Keith shrugged his shoulders.

"It's easy when the person betrays you and has no desire to make it better."

"Good seeing you, Keith. I hope everything works out for you."

I headed to the register as Keith continued to stroll the aisles, looking for the perfect movie.

Papa John's never disappoints. My spinach and cheese pizza hit the spot. Beyoncé gave a stellar performance in the movie, but the girl who played Effie was phenomenal. Jennifer Hudson may not have been the winner of American Idol, but she was giving rising star vibes in this movie.

I hadn't spoken with Mimi in a while, so I decided to call and fill her in on my disastrous life. Mimi was left speechless outside of the whores, bitches, and tricks she called Samone.

"I'm glad you called, Sharae. I was thinking of moving. How is Virginia outside of your drama?"

"Virginia has a nice feel to it. I enjoy it here."

Mimi went on to tell me that she was resigning from Westside Elementary. Her boss's wife found out about them and threatened to blast their relationship if she didn't end it. I was surprised that Mimi was giving up so easily and even considering leaving her mom.

"You're welcome here, Mimi. There are plenty of teaching jobs, and this house is too big for little old me."

Before Mimi and I hung up, she decided that she would become a Virginia resident at the beginning of February. I felt some relief knowing that I would have someone I loved in the same city as me.

The rest of January was a blur. I went to work, but nothing excited me, not even closing seven-figure deals. Jamal distanced himself from me, except for a business conversation.

Today was going to be a good day. Mimi was finally making her debut in Virginia. I heard the music before I ever saw her car. I knew it was Mimi. The song *Low* by FloRida was bumping from her speakers. Mimi may have originally been from New York, but she was the epitome of a Florida girl.

I ran to greet her as she got out of her car, a black-on-black G35 Infiniti with cold black rims. Yeah, Mimi was a Florida girl. She hopped out of the car with blonde micro braids hanging down her back.

"Girl! It is cold out here. Is it like this all day?" Mimi yelled as we lugged her belongings into her new home.

"Yeah, the weather doesn't begin to break until around May. You'll get used to experiencing the different seasons and creating a winter wardrobe."

I showed Mimi around the house. She was in love.

"So, you mean to tell me that Jamal just gave you this house? Say you swear you haven't given him any of Miss Kitty."

"I swear, well, he's tasted it."

I blushed as I thought of how Jamal would devour me. He acted as if it were the last supper every time.

"What's wrong with him? Why isn't he your man?"

"Nothing is wrong with him. Remember Brenton, the love of my life, my first, the man who was supposed to protect me and love me beyond himself? I guess life has a way of showing you who's who."

"So now what, Sharae? You're single, and you have a man who loves you. A man who wants you and only you. I wish I had that."

Mimi looked away from me. I assumed she was thinking of her boss. I didn't know much about dating married men, but my godmother would always tell me that there was no future in someone else's man. I guess it was for Samone.

Mimi and I talked into the wee hours of the morning and fell asleep in my plush-size bed, just like when we were kids, and she was escaping her home life. I noticed a bruise on the back of Mimi's arm. She told me that her boss had grabbed her before she left because she refused to have farewell sex with him. The audacity of him! I told Mimi that I wasn't interested in being with anyone right now. I needed to figure myself out as a grown woman. I've never done anything alone or just for me. The time is now.

***

The weekend passed quickly. Mimi and I did a little sightseeing, mainly at all of the malls. We hit up Greenbrier, Lynnhaven, and McArthur malls. McArthur Mall has an ice-skating park during the winter months. I convinced Mimi that we should try it out. Mimi and I paid for our tickets and laced up our ice skates. We held on to the walls of the rink until a guy came and grabbed our hands. He pulled us along as we glided on his sides. Mimi got the hang of ice skating quicker than me and was scooting on her own. I decided to let the stranger's hand go and go back to pulling myself along the sides of the rink.

Boom! There was a loud sound, and as I looked back, I saw the stranger who helped us before helping Mimi to her feet. After Mimi's big bang, we decided to head to Military Circle Mall. Military Circle was more of what we were used to. It was more urban. The author, Kiki Swinson, was there doing a book signing at Barnes and Noble. I got an autographed copy of her book, *Wifey*. My mom instilled a love for reading in me at an early age, but I realized I hadn't read as much lately. This was the first step in getting back to me.

Genesis

10

Mimi secured a job at Crestwood Intermediate as a fifth-grade teacher. She loved every minute of it. She was truly born to be a teacher. The passion Mimi has for children is undeniable, and the kids love her.

I hadn't spoken with Brenton since I left. Initially, I was heartbroken and would cry myself to sleep. I had a recurring dream that Brenton and I were together. We had a baby girl, but every time I looked in the bassinet, I saw Samone's face. No more Princess Jasmine.

The sun was shining brightly today. I was doing an open house in the Dam Neck area of Virginia Beach. It was a rare warm day in March. So many couples had come in with big smiles on their faces. They were all ready to begin the American Dream. The last couple pulled up in a white SUV that still had paper tags. I was hoping this wasn't a new purchase for them because that wouldn't look good on their credit if they were trying to purchase it.

The man walked to the passenger side door

and opened it for who I assumed was his wife. Her belly got out before she did. I smiled. Starting a family is still a goal of mine. My smile turned into disgust once I noticed it was Samone and Brenton. Samone wore a yellow jumpsuit that was tied around her neck. She waddled, looking as if she was ready to deliver at any minute. Brenton was still as fine as ever and hadn't missed any gym days. His Florida swag was apparent. He was wearing khaki cargo pants, a Ralph Lauren Polo shirt, and a pair of Air Max 95s.

They both walked towards the house. I wanted to scream. Samone extended her hand, and we shook. I offered them some of the snacks that were provided and gave them the liberty to tour the house. I began to clean up as the other couples left. Samone and Brenton made their way back to me, enthused.

"This is our house, Sharae. We want it."

Samone talked to me as if we were old friends, and not that she was standing next to the man she stole from me.

"Are we really doing this?"

I had to ask because at this point I knew Ashton Kutcher was going to jump out and tell me I was being Punk'd. Brenton began to speak.

"Yes, we're doing this. Now grow up and get your commission."

"Can you even afford this home? And what's with the new SUV? That wasn't a smart move for someone looking to buy a home."

"Well, my parents bought us this car to help jump-start our future," Samone interjected.

I noticed her ring. It sat perfectly on her left hand. It was nothing compared to the ring Jamal had given me, but it was not chopped liver.

"When is the wedding?"

There was a lump in my throat.

"August 23rd. I want to have time to get into my wedding dress."

I could hear Jamal's voice in my head, saying, "Don't be naive about the situation."

Brenton may not have set all of this up, but Samone sure did. There was a gush of water that came from between Samone's legs.

"Oh my gosh, my water broke!"

"It can't be. You still have four more weeks."

Brenton paced frantically. I stood in a daze as Samone slid to the floor. She began to scream, and her breathing was fast.

"The baby is coming."

I grabbed my phone and dialed 911. Brenton placed Samone's head on his lap. The 911 operator began to coach me on what to do. Samone spread her legs. I pulled off her panties and to my surprise, the baby's head was right there. Samone took deep breaths and pushed. It seemed like an eternity, but after about five pushes, the baby was here.

The baby cried and just in time the ambulance pulled up. I moved out of the way as they helped Brenton cut the umbilical cord. Samone had to push some more, and this bloody little sac came out. Samone's eyes began to roll to the back of her head, and she began to bleed profusely. The paramedics put her on the gurney, got her and the baby into the back of the ambulance, and headed to the hospital.

I looked at Brenton. He was sobbing. I grabbed his hand and led him to my car. I drove as fast as I could to Virginia Beach General Hospital. We didn't speak while on our way. We pulled in shortly after the ambulance. Two nurses came out and escorted Brenton and me to a small room. Still no words. After about thirty minutes, a short, female doctor who looked to be in her early thirties came in.

"I'm sorry to say, but the mother didn't make it."

Brenton collapsed. I asked about the baby and was informed that he was doing fine. They had a boy. A nurse came in to help Brenton to a chair and took his vital signs. He was going to be okay.

"Can I see my son?" Brenton asked with a shaky voice.

I walked with Brenton to the nursery. Wrapped in a little blanket and hat, Baby Brothers looked our way with bright brown eyes.

"What's his name?"

"Genesis Liam Brothers," Brenton spoke, holding back tears.

"The beginning," I thought to myself.

There was no need for a DNA test. Genesis had Brenton's nose and eyes. He was a perfect shade of brown with a head full of hair, just like Samone. The nurse motioned for Brenton and me to come inside the nursery. Brenton sat in a white rocking chair, and the nurse placed Genesis on his chest. I stood next to Brenton as he rocked back and forth, holding the back of his baby boy's head. Genesis wasn't a small baby. On his bassinet, his weight and height read 9lbs. 2oz., and 20 inches.

"Do you want to hold him?"

I was shocked by Brenton's question. I did want to hold Genesis, but I couldn't. I thought about the babies that I didn't have the strength to keep. After Samone's death, I felt jealous of her. Whether her motive was to steal my fiancé or not, she had the strength to do what I didn't, even though it killed her.

After a few hours, I drove Brenton back to the home where he and Samone were going to build their family. We walked into the home and were stopped by Samone's blood, which began to stain the floor. Brenton ran out to his SUV. I looked out to see him at the steering wheel, sobbing. I grabbed some cleaning supplies out of my trunk. On my hands and knees, I scrubbed the floor until all traces of Samone were gone. I followed Brenton back to our apartment.

Brenton called Samone's parents. They were devastated by the news but promised to be active in Genesis' life and plan the funeral. Next, Brenton called his parents, and they were equally encouraging. Mrs. Brothers said she would catch a flight the following day to welcome baby Genesis. Lastly, Brenton called Keith and told him of the birth and death. Keith was speechless but insisted he still wanted a DNA test. Brenton didn't fight with him about it. I went into the kitchen and found some ground turkey thawing in the sink. I cooked spaghetti, corn on the cob, and garlic bread. I fixed Brenton's plate, and we ate in silence.

"I have to get the baby's room together. Samone and I planned on moving before he arrived, so we didn't put anything together."

I told Brenton I would help him. We stayed up until 3:00 a.m. building dressers, constructing the crib, making sure the bassinet was sturdy, and placing the jungle decor Samone picked out. I unpacked Genesis's clothes and placed them in the closet and drawers. I stacked the diapers next to the wipe warmer and diaper genie. The room was perfect. I wanted to stay and console Brenton, but I couldn't. He chose Samone. He chose Genesis, and her death doesn't change the fact that he didn't choose me.

"Good night, Brenton. I'll always love you, and I wish you the best."

I drove to Chesapeake with uncontrollable tears falling from my eyes. Usher's hit song, *Burn*, played on the radio. I cried even more. I pulled into the driveway and noticed Jamal's car was parked behind Mimi's.

Mimi and Jamal were sleeping on separate couches in the back living room. They both woke up once I turned on the light. There were UNO cards and a pizza box on the floor next to a bottle of Jack Daniels. It looks like they had a fun night.

Jamal spoke first.

"Hey, Sharae, I've been waiting for you."

"Yeah, it looks like you had an enjoyable wait," I responded sarcastically.

"Don't do that, Sharae. Jamal stopped by for you, but you never showed up, so I chilled with him. No big deal. Where were you, by the way?"

Mimi had all of the answers. I explained everything that happened. Mimi and Jamal both sat with their mouths open. There was a moment of silence before I started to cry again. Jamal hugged me tightly. I led him to our bedroom. I undressed and got into the shower. I tried to scrub the stench of the hospital and the smell of Samone's blood off of my skin. I cried some more. There was a suffocating feeling in my chest. The water felt brisk as I slid my back against the shower wall. Jamal wrapped me in a towel, carried me out of the shower, and laid me on the bed. He lotioned my body with a slight massage, just like my mommy did when I was feeling sick as a little girl. I fell asleep.

The next morning, Jamal was still there. Mimi had already gone to work. Jamal made me coffee, but I drank orange juice instead and ate half a bagel.

"Sharae, you know you aren't obligated to

Brenton or his baby, right?" Jamal spoke with sincerity in his voice.

"I know, and I don't want to be. I still stand against becoming a mother at 23. I didn't choose my kids. How can I choose someone else's?"

I know God forgave me for my abortions, but the birth of Genesis is making guilt arise in my heart.

"What age do you want to become a mother?"

"I really never thought about an age. I've always thought about being financially stable. I want to give my child the life my dad gave me. We weren't rich, but I never needed anything, and I got everything I wanted if it made sense."

My dad was a great provider. My parents had a perfect balance. My dad was the breadwinner, but he still showed up physically for me and never made my mom feel bad for not providing financially.

"You have that now, Sharae. You are doing well financially, and with me, there is no uncertainty with finances. When you're ready, I'm ready."

I don't know what it was about me that Jamal needed so badly. I believe in myself, but he treated me as if God had created me just for him.

"Jamal, I'm ready for us to date. How we started was unorthodox, and I am ready to give just US a try."

"I'd like that."

Jamal hugged me from behind and rested his chin on my head. I felt safe. This is my Genesis.

11

A few weeks passed, and I hadn't heard from Brenton. I knew his mom and Samone's parents were supporting him and that he didn't need me. I kind of hated that he didn't need me, but it was a reality. I decided to give him a call.

"Hey Brenton, how are you and baby Genesis?"

"We're doing good. I'm trying to adjust to my mom and Samone's mom no longer being here. They did everything for him. I'm on paternity leave, so I have about 5 more weeks to get in the groove of things."

I listened to Brenton talk with calmness. This was the Brenton that I had fallen in love with.

"Has Keith taken the DNA test?"

Something in my heart hoped that Genesis was Keith's son.

"He did, and the boy is mine."

Brenton and I both laughed as we connected his response with the hit song by Brandy and Monica. There was a moment of silence. I always imagined Brenton and I starting a family.

"Brenton, you're going to be a great dad. Trust God through all of this."

I was surprised at my response. I hadn't talked to God in a while. I wonder if He has forgotten about me.

"Thanks, Sharae. I was wondering if you would be Genesis' Godmother. What do you think? I know this is awkward, but I also know that you'll be great."

"I can't Brenton. I don't want to. I don't want to be connected to someone that I feel like ripped my family apart. Genesis is innocent, but he is the product of Samone."

"I understand Sharae, but just know that the position is open. I have also been trusting God through all of this. Your dad has been counseling me and helping me find my way back to our savior."

I hung up the phone with Brenton and began to cry again. It seemed like all I did was cry these days. I went into my bedroom and searched my oversized closet for some running shoes. Running was a thing of the past, but I remember my mother telling me before she passed that who you truly are will always be deep inside of you.

Tucked in a corner were my Avia running sneakers. They looked a bit worn, similar to my life.

The air was cool. After a short stretch, I began to run, first starting with a light jog and increasing into a full sprint. Before I knew it, 30 minutes had passed, and I was running up to my doorstep. I sat on the steps. I don't remember much of the scenery as I ran, but I did remember every part of my life after my mom died. It was tough for my dad and me, but my dad's faith got us through. His faith helped me develop my faith. Somewhere along the way, I guess I forgot who my source was. I looked for it in Brenton, track, real estate, Mimi, and, as of lately, Jamal.

I checked my watch and noticed there were 45 minutes before church would start. I hadn't visited church since Jamal's invitation, but my soul was calling for healing. I was skeptical about visiting the church I went to with Jamal because I wanted an intimate feel of God and didn't know if I could receive that at a megachurch, but I decided that God would show up wherever I welcomed him.

I dressed in all black as if I were going to a funeral. I felt dead inside. At the end of the service, the pastor asked if anyone needed to be restored and, if so, come to the altar. My feet moved before I could talk myself out of it. I stood at the altar, and my head was anointed with oil. I raised my hands and began to call the name of Jesus. I could feel the presence of the Lord. A warm hand touched my back as a soft voice whispered in my ear for me to surrender. I surrendered to God and rededicated my life to him. A woman embraced me with a hug. I opened my eyes to see Mrs. Carter with tears streaming down her face.

I went back to my seat, and as the pastor was giving the benediction, he stated that the Lord was telling him to have a baptism today. I was baptized as a little girl, but honestly, only because I was the preacher's daughter. I got baptized again this Sunday. The Carters (including Jamal) invited me over for lunch after service. On the car ride, I called my dad and told him about my experience. He couldn't stop thanking God for saving me.

"Baby girl, I've been praying that you were set free. God still answers prayers."

"Thank you, Daddy, for never giving up on me."

I hung up from my dad as I arrived at the Carter's estate. The landscaping was breathtaking. To the left of the house, three horses were grazing the perfectly maintained lawn. I never knew anyone who owned horses. I rode a horse in Jamaica, but that's about it.

"Welcome," Mrs. Carter greeted me at the door and led me into the family room.

Everything was simple in the Carters' home - nothing unnecessary. Just like their vacation home in Hawaii, all of the rooms were white, with a pop of color here and there.

"Thank you for having me."

I don't know why I felt tense around Mrs. Carter. Well, I guess it's because she told me not to hurt her son, and I have done the exact opposite. I was expecting to have a chef-prepared meal, but Mrs. Carter had prepared the entire dinner before the church service. The spread included some of my favorite dishes: oxtails, beans and rice, collard greens, and cornbread that melted in my mouth.

"Mrs. Carter, everything is so delicious."

"Thank you. My mother taught me everything that I know, and I taught my boys."

Mrs. Carter looked at Jamal with a twinkle in her eyes. Guilt rose inside of me for having abortions, knowing that the Carters' oldest son was taken away.

"Mom, Sharae and I are officially dating."

Mr. Carter, a man of few words, interjected, "What happened to your boyfriend, Sharae? Is my son some type of rebound guy?"

I shifted in my seat. "No, sir, Jamal and I have been very cautious about giving ourselves a title. We are both ready to explore what a relationship will look like. My ex, Brenton, chose a different path that didn't include me."

"So, my son is the second choice?" Mr. Carter didn't even blink with his questioning.

"Dad, give Sharae a break. This isn't 21 questions."

"Let the young lady answer," Mr. Carter kept his eyes on me.

I looked directly into Mr. Carter's eyes and said, "No, sir, Jamal is not the second choice. If I had met him earlier in my life, I would have no ex, but that's not how life works. God allowed us to meet when the timing was right."

"Okay, enough of the interrogation, Dad."

Jamal stood up from the table and asked if we could be excused. I admired their family structure. Mrs. Carter excused us.

Jamal led me to the backyard. As much land as the Carters' estate sat on, I wasn't even sure if I should call this a backyard. Jamal and I sat on a white tree swing, swinging back and forth. I snuggled my head in the nape of Jamal's neck. I felt safe. My spirit was renewed, and a sense of peace was over me. Jamal grabbed my left hand and slipped my engagement ring on my finger. He stopped the swing and looked directly into my eyes.

"Sharae, what God has for me and you separately is great, but what he has for us together is beyond our wildest dreams. I want to experience God's promise with you. Will you marry me?"

"Yes, Jamal, yes, I'll marry you." Jamal and I kissed like they do in the Lifetime movies - overly dramatic.

Jamal and I ran into the house to share the news with his parents. Mrs. Carter was delighted. Mr. Carter gave his blessing, but not without a warning.

"Young love is beautiful but will come with many tests. Make sure you both pass the test."

Jamal and Mr. Carter embraced each other as I dialed my dad's number. I began to tell my dad the good news. He didn't seem as enthused as me, but he told me that he trusted God. As I was hanging up, the doorbell rang. Jamal opened the door.

"Alex!"

There stood Jamal's ex. She looked to be a little taller than me, with high yellow skin and a shape that reminded me of the video vixen, Melissa Ford.

"Hi, Jamal."

Alex's voice was soft. I guess I'm not the only one who called Lucky, Jamal.

"Can I come in?"

"Uh, sure," Jamal fumbled over his words. Mr. and Mrs. Carter came into the foyer, and they both looked at Alex with disappointment. As Jamal began to close the door behind Alex, a little girl who looked to be six or seven years old squeezed in behind her. We locked eyes, and she looked just like Princess Jasmine.

We all went into the family room. Jamal introduced me as his fiancé, and Alex introduced the little girl, Jada, as Jamal's daughter. The room was silent until Mrs. Carter spoke.

"We'll need a DNA test."

Alex agreed without hesitation.

"Once the DNA results come back. I am relinquishing my parental rights," Alex spoke without feeling or regard for the fact that Jada was sitting next to her.

"My fiancé doesn't want children. He plays football for the Atlanta Falcons, and I'll be moving to Atlanta once all of these legalities are resolved. Jada is a great kid. She's always asked about you. I kept her from you because we never discussed being parents. I went to have an abortion, but I was too far along, and Jameson had passed away during the same time frame. Please forgive me, but I have to make this selfish decision to live the life that I desire."

Alex was heartless. I moved closer to Jamal and rubbed his back, the same way that Caprice would rub my father's back in uncomfortable situations.

"After the DNA test, I will take full responsibility if Jada is mine."

Jamal looked at me as he spoke. I looked into his eyes with reassurance. I'm not sure why my heart or mind didn't tell me to run; instead, I heard a voice telling me that Jada would need me just like I needed a mother at seven years old.

God's Plan

12

The Wednesday after meeting Jada, Jamal and Jada had a DNA test performed. Jamal paid extra for rapid results, so within 48 hours, Jamal learned that he was Jada's father. Without hesitation, Alex dropped Jada off at the home, which Jamal and I now shared. Mimi answered the door.

"You must be Jada. I'm your Aunt Mimi. I hope you like princess stuff because Ms. Sharae has overloaded your room with pink and princess."

Jada smiled as Mimi led her to the bedroom.

Alex handed Jamal Jada's information: a birth certificate, social security, and insurance cards. She told him that the insurance would end because it's Medicaid, and she wouldn't qualify for that anymore.

"Jada!" Alex yelled Jada's name.

Jada ran from the backroom. "Yes. ma'am?"

"You're safe here with your dad and Ms. Sharae. You can call me anytime that you like, and we can even Skype. I love you."

Alex kissed Jada's forehead and walked out

the door. We all stood silently. Jamal had a look of hopelessness on his face. I felt confused. How could Jamal and I parent a child together if we've never experienced each other sexually?

Jada poked me in the side. I looked down at her.

"Yes, Jada?"

"I'm hungry. Do you know how to cook?"

Her face and words were so innocent. In that moment, I understood that what I desired was not what God planned for me.

"I sure do know how to cook. What are you thinking we should have for dinner?"

"My mom always makes fried chicken on Fridays. Can we have fried chicken?"

"Absolutely, would you like to go to the grocery store with me?"

Jada said yes and started to slip on her shoes. I grabbed my shoes. Jamal handed me his credit card and embraced me tightly.

Jamal whispered in my ear, "Thank you."

I matched his grip and kissed his neck. Jamal told Jada to pick out her favorite snacks, and Jada informed us that she is allergic to strawberries. That is something Alex should have told us. Good thing Jada knew how to speak up for herself.

Jada buckled herself into the backseat of my car. I adjusted my rear-view mirror, and my eyes connected with Jada's eyes.

In a low voice, Jada mustered up, "Are you

my mommy?"

My heart did a cartwheel, and I thought about all the times I said I wasn't ready to be a mother, how I didn't want to raise someone else's kid, and then I thought of all the times I dreamt of Princess Jasmine.

"Yes, Jada, I am your mommy."

We both smiled. It felt as if the sun was shining directly on me, almost blinding. I knew then that God was still with me, just like he was with me when I was seven years old and motherless.

About the Author

Meet Santina S. Proctor

Santina is a native of Daytona Beach, Florida, and now resides in Chesapeake, Virginia, with her husband and children. She is an author and a Certified Professional Mindset Coach, however at one time she was just a woman searching for balance and unsure of her purpose.

As a wife, mother, and career woman, life became overwhelming for Santina. With God, determination, and guidance she was able to reach her full potential. She has encountered many life experiences as a U.S. Army veteran, serving in Operation Enduring Freedom and working 18 years as a Licensed Practical Nurse. She has helped cultivate our future by working for four years as a 7th grade ELA teacher.

Santina is the founder of the non-profit organization, *It's Not Your Fault 91, Inc.* which brings resources and awareness to domestic violence. She is the author of ***It's Already Yours, Go Get It***, and ***It's not a Vacation, it's a Lifestyle***. Each experience has created an opportunity for Santina to align with her purpose; her survival is the key to your success.